Contents

Series Reading Consultant: Prue Goodwin
Reading and Language Information Centre,
University of Reading

Chapter One

As the children arrived at the village school, they gazed proudly at the long, colourful banner hanging above the main door.

"It looks brilliant!" cried Hannah.

"It should do," said Tom. "We spent ages painting it."

Rebecca sighed. "I'll be very
sad if our little school really has
to close."

"No more school . . ." Tom said dreamily. "I could stay in bed all day!"

"They won't let you do that," Rebecca said, pulling a face. "We'd have to go to that big horrible school in town instead."

"By bus!" Hannah said in disgust. "Yuk!"

Michael came into the
playground to ring the bell.
CLANG! CLANG! DING!
DONG!

"OK, OK, Michael, we've heard it," Tom grinned. "I reckon you've woken up the whole of Great Catesby by now."

The small group of seven- and eight-year-olds sat on the carpet around their teacher.

"We're going to have a new boy in our class today," Mrs Roberts told them. "He wasn't very happy at his old school, so let's make sure that he will like it here with us."

Michael put his hand up. "He won't be here for long if the place is gonna close soon!" he said cheekily.

The teacher frowned at him. "We'll all be doing our best to stop that from happening."

"But how can we stop it?" Hannah blurted out.

"It won't be easy," Mrs Roberts admitted. "But we mustn't give up hope of finding a way to save our lovely school."

Rebecca couldn't help bursting into song. It was the latest hit single by her favourite pop star, the Red Fox.

"*Never give up, never give up,*
 Stop your crying, you gotta keep
on trying,
 Something will turn up – will
always turn up . . ."

The others joined in the
chorus.
 "*Something will turn up – will*
always turn up . . ."

Something did at that very
moment. With the children in
full voice, the classroom door
was pushed open and Miss
Jackson, the headteacher,
walked in.

The song faded away as, one by one, they stared at the little boy with ginger hair standing next to her. He had a football tucked under his arm.

"I wish you would all sing as well as that in assembly," Miss Jackson said with  a smile and then introduced their new classmate. "This is Jonty. Say hello, everyone."

The boy gave them a wide, toothy grin and the ice was broken.

"Hello, Jonty!" they chorused.
"Hi!" he beamed, and
suddenly bounced the ball on
the floor. "Anybody here like to
play football?"

They all laughed. "Welcome, Jonty," Mrs Roberts greeted him warmly. "It seems like you've come to the right place. This lot of mine are totally soccer-mad."

Chapter Two

Jonty's arrival at Great Catesby was well timed. Mrs Roberts was planning to enter a class team in a five-a-side football tournament especially for their age-group.

"You live in that big house outside the village, don't you?" Michael said to him one day. "Are your parents rich?"

Jonty gave a shrug. "Haven't got a mum. And Dad's away a lot. I don't see much of him."

"Who looks after you then?" asked Rebecca, trying to work out what it was about Jonty that seemed so familiar to her.

"Gran does," he said. "And we've got a housekeeper too."

"I'd rather be a goalkeeper!" grinned Hannah.

The first practice for the Fives
was held later that week
Most of the class took part,
hoping to be picked for the
team.

"It will be mixed, won't it?" asked Hannah. "Girls too."

"Of course," said Mrs Roberts. "You're our best goalie."

"Out of all the girls, maybe," Imran whispered to Tom. "But not the best in the whole class. That's me."

"You'll have to prove it, Imran," Tom smirked. "She's good."

Jonty took his own leather
ball to the practice and he was
the first one to score with it as
well. His shot was low and hard
and the ball fizzed just out of
reach of Hannah's dive.

 Hannah
more upset by
Imran's laughter
at the other end
than she was at letting the goal
in. And she soon made up for it.
She saved another effort from
Jonty and then stopped a close-
range header from Tom on the
line.

Hannah threw the ball out to
Rebecca on the wing to start
their own team's next attack.

Rebecca had won the sprint
race on Sports Day and was too
quick for anyone to catch her,
even running with the ball at
her feet.

She curled the ball over into the goalmouth, but it floated right into Imran's arms. Or at least it should have done. Imran took his eye off the ball at the last moment and let it slip between his legs into the goal. He was so embarrassed, he held his head in his hands.

"Careful, Imran!" yelled Tom.
"You might drop that too!"

Imran decided he didn't want
to play in goal after all. He was
better out on the pitch as a
defender.

When the practice finished,
Rebecca had a sudden
brainwave. "Why don't we ask
people to sponsor us in the
Fives?" she suggested. "We
could raise a lot of money for
the school."

"Great idea!" said Tom. "But
what about kit? We can't all
wear different colours."

"That is a problem," agreed
Mrs Roberts. "I'm afraid the
school can't afford to buy a
team strip."

"I'll see if my dad might be able to help," Jonty piped up, making himself even more popular. "He's a big football fan."

Rebecca nodded. "I bet that's not all he is either," she said under her breath.

A wild rumour had begun to snake around the village that a famous pop star had recently moved into the area. Nobody thought that it could possibly be true — apart from Rebecca . . .

Chapter Three

The children could not believe
their eyes. A man with bright
red hair had just walked into
their classroom.

But it wasn't his hair colour that gave them such a shock. It was because they recognized him. He was the Red Fox!

Only Mrs Roberts and Jonty were expecting his visit.

The Red Fox was holding a large cardboard box. "Got some stuff here for all you star footballers," he said with a grin.

The pop star tipped the box upside down and lots of soccer kit tumbled out on to the floor.

He grabbed one of the red shirts
and held it up for everyone to
see.

It had a big white capital G
on the front and the name
GREATS printed across the
back above the number.

"G is for Great – and that's what you'll be in the Fives!" he cried before breaking into a chant. *"C'mon, you Greats! C'mon, you Greats!"*

The children were still too
stunned to know what to do
until Rebecca joined in and
then the rest followed. Their
loud chanting echoed around
the school – and probably
halfway around Great Catesby
as well.

*"C'mon, you Greats! C'mon,
you Greats!"*

When the Red Fox had gone,
Jonty was surrounded.

"Is he really your dad?" Tom
demanded. "You could have
told us!"

Jonty smiled shyly. "I wanted

to keep it a secret for a while. I hoped you wouldn't all be friends with me just because of who my dad is."

"With your name being Fox and your ginger hair, we should have guessed," said Hannah.

"I already did," Rebecca
claimed. "And last night I found
I've even got a picture of Jonty
in my Red Fox scrapbook. I
knew I'd seen him somewhere
before."

"Becky's fallen in love with
Jonty!" Imran teased her.
Rebecca ignored him.

"Incredible!" she sighed. "I've just been singing along with the Red Fox!"

"He's only Jonty's dad," Imran sneered.

"*Only!*" she sneered back. "He's the best pop singer in the world."

"Well, my dad sings pretty well too – in the bath."

"Yeah, but I don't have a poster of your dad on my bedroom wall," she laughed. "Especially not one of him in the bath!"

★

After another soccer practice, Mrs Roberts chose a squad of six players for the tournament so that they had a substitute for each game. She wrote the names on the entry form.

FIVE-A-SIDE COMPETITION
- Entry Form -
Tom (captain) Hannah Rebecca
Jonty Michael Imran

The whole school had a special reason for hoping that the team did well. The Red Fox was so pleased by how quickly Jonty had settled in that he was sponsoring the Greats too.

Not just for a few pence per goal. Not even for a pound a goal like some generous people in the village. But for as much as a thousand pounds for every goal that they scored!

Jonty's only disappointment was that his dad wouldn't be able to watch them play in the Fives. He was setting off on a concert tour with his band.

"I'll be thinking of you, Jonty-boy," his dad promised before he left. "Show 'em who's the soccer star of the Fox family."

Jonty managed a weak smile.

"I really like it at this school, Dad. If it's closed, I might have to go back to that horrible boarding school where I was bullied."

"There'll be no going back there, don't worry. I'll see to that, OK?"

"*C'mon, you Greats!*" they sang happily together.

Chapter Four

"Fantastic! We're in the quarter-finals now," cried Tom.

The captain's second goal
had just clinched his team's 2–0
victory, their third win in a row.

The Greats were enjoying themselves so much, they'd almost forgotten about all the money they were earning for the school.

"Wish my dad could have been here to see us," said Jonty.

There was a sudden stir of excitement in the crowd as a helicopter began to circle overhead. It looked as if it was going to land on the playing fields.

It did. Everyone felt the gusts
of wind from the whirling
blades, and then a red-haired
figure in a white suit stepped
down from the helicopter and
ran towards them.

The Red Fox was soon surrounded by autograph-hunters.

"Hope I'm not too late," he called out to the Greats.

Inspired by his flying visit, they hit top form and the red shirts swarmed all over their opponents in the next match.

Goals from Rebecca, Michael
and Jonty swept them easily into
the semi-finals.

"*C'mon, you
Greats!*" cheered
their fans, led
by the Red
Fox himself. He
jumped nearly as high as his
helicopter when Jonty scored the
third goal!

 "You're costing me a fortune," he laughed, clearly not minding one little bit.

The semi-final game was much tougher. The score was locked at 0–0 until the last minute, and that's when Hannah pulled off a magnificent save to rescue her team.

A goal looked certain. A shot was deflected off Imran's knee, but Hannah twisted round and hurled herself through the air to fingertip the ball over the crossbar.

"What a save!" cried Imran. "Thanks, Hannah. I take back all I've said. You're magic in goal!"

Tom headed the corner out of danger towards Rebecca and the Greats launched a swift breakaway raid. As Rebecca raced up the pitch, Jonty matched her for pace and he burst past his marker to reach her pass first. He smacked the ball from just outside the keeper's area and it screamed into the goal.

Jonty disappeared under a pile of teammates as they mobbed him. Only Hannah stayed out of the crush of bodies.

"We're in the Final!" she yelled. "We've made it!"

★

There wasn't much time for the players to rest before the Final, but they were too excited to feel tired yet. They were up against the tournament favourites, the Fab Five, a strong team from the biggest school in the county.

The Greats didn't care who they were playing. They rocked the Fab Five straight from the kick-off when Imran's long-range shot whistled only a fraction wide of the target. And

with a little luck, they might
have been leading by more than
1–0 at half-time. Rebecca
scored their goal, sliding home
the rebound after Tom's volley
had struck a post.

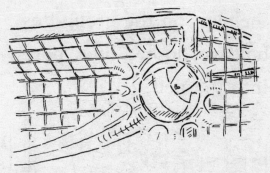

The second half, sadly, told a
different story. Once the Fab
Five had equalized, the Greats
struggled to survive a storm of
fierce attacks. Just when it

looked like they might hang on for a draw, their defence was finally cracked.

Not even Hannah could keep out the winning goal. She'd already blocked one shot and was helpless on the ground as the ball was lashed back past her into the net.

"Never mind," said Mrs Roberts after the squad received their silver medals as runners-up. "You all played your best and nobody can ask for more than that."

"But we didn't win," sighed Rebecca, almost in tears, despite the fact that they'd scored a total of ten goals.

"Cheer up!"said the Red Fox. "There's always another day."

"Not for our school, there won't be," grunted Tom.

The pop star began to sing.

"Never give up, never give up, Something will turn up, will always turn up . . ."

"I know what can turn up, Dad," cried Jonty. "A song! Why don't you make a record with all the kids at Great Catesby? That could raise loads more money to help save the school."

Everyone thought that was a wonderful idea – including the Red Fox. He ruffled his son's ginger hair.

"Right, let's do it, Jonty-boy," he grinned. "If it did the trick, it'd be an even greater save than Hannah's!"

Jonty started up their chant again and the footballers really had something to sing about now. Mrs Roberts laughed in delight. "It sounds like we've got the title for our song already!"

"*C'mon, you Greats! C'mon, you Greats!*"

THE END